3-04-2022

To all those four-legged creatures who are looking for a home, and to those who open their hearts and homes in giving them one. I would like to thank Caring Canines and Dogs on Call in Richmond, Virginia, for allowing us the opportunity to show how special Webster was.

A percentage of proceeds from this book will go to the following organizations:

- **The MCV Children's Hospital in Richmond, Virginia**

- **Homeless Animal Protection, Placement & Education (HAPPE)** – an all-volunteer, non-profit dog rescue group located in Richmond, Virginia

- **Peaceful Passings Senior Animal Rescue** - a non-profit retirement home for elderly and handicapped dogs in Charlottesville, Virginia

www.mascotbooks.com

Webster the Beagle

For more information, please contact:
Mascot Books
620 Herndon Parkway #320
Herndon, VA 20170
info@mascotbooks.com

Library of Congress Control Number: 2018903418

CPSIA Code: PRT0518A
ISBN-13: 978-1-68401-830-7

Printed in the United States

WEBSTER

the Beagle

written by Frank Payne

illustrated by Romney Vasquez

Webster the beagle was born in Virginia to a family of eight other beagles. He lived outdoors with his family in a small doghouse called a kennel. There were lots of other dogs living there too because it was a kennel for hunting dogs.

Being a hunting dog meant Webster had to go out with the hunters and all the other dogs and chase after animals all day. It wasn't his favorite thing to do. Webster didn't want to be a hunting dog. He wanted to play instead!

Living with so many other dogs meant that Webster had to fight for food every day. Every night, he had to search and search to find a place to sleep.

Some days Webster got very little food, and some nights he had to sleep outside in the cold of winter or the heat of summer.

One day while hunting with the other dogs in the woods, Webster got separated from his pack. He had no idea where he was, and he tried and tried to find his way home.

For two long days, he wandered through the woods with no food, lost and alone. Sleeping in the woods was even worse than sleeping in the kennel.

On the third day, Webster saw something familiar. A hunter! He ran as fast as he could toward him and jumped in his lap, kissing his face in excitement.

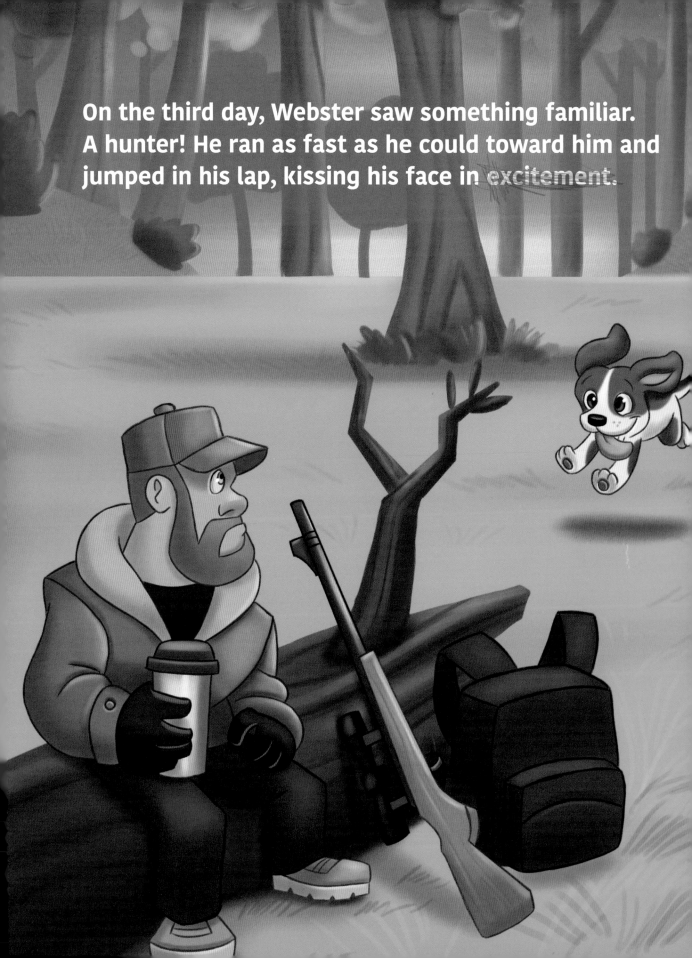

The hunter couldn't believe it! He had never seen a hunting dog act that way. He quickly realized that this beagle was special. He was hunting for a family, not an animal!

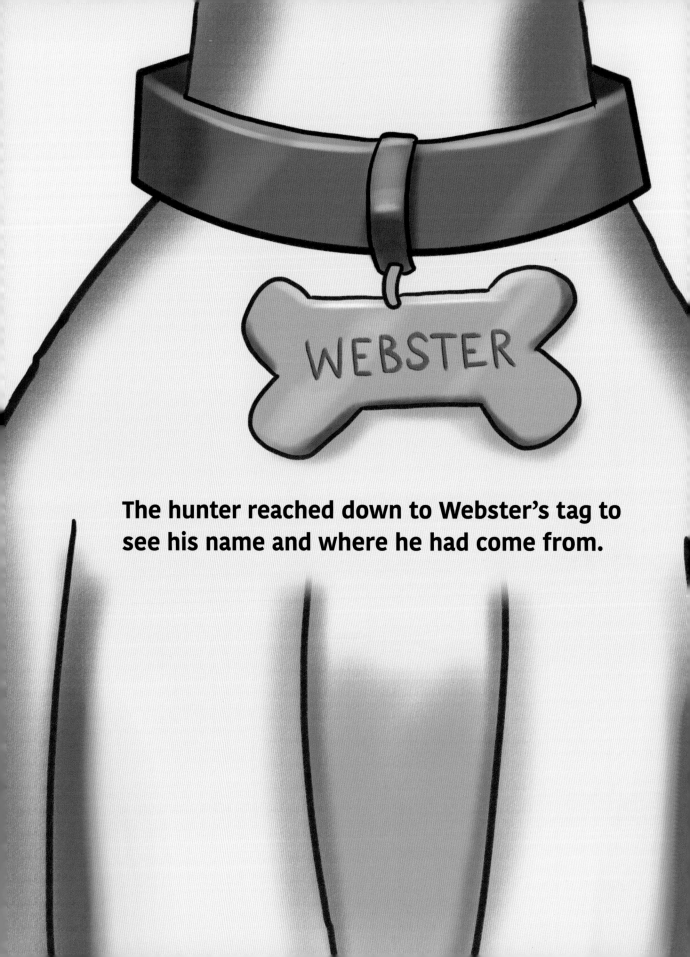

The hunter reached down to Webster's tag to see his name and where he had come from.

The hunter knew he wasn't going to see any other
animals that day because they'd all smell Webster
on him from a mile away, so he decided to head
back to the kennel with Webster at his heels. He
knew he had to return him to his kennel.

After the hunter dropped Webster off, he headed home. But he couldn't stop thinking about that little beagle and how happy he was when he jumped in his lap and how sad he was when he took him back to the kennel.

He knew he had to do something, so he turned his truck around and headed back for his beagle!

The hunter went right up to the kennel owner and asked what it would take to bring Webster home with him. Turns out, two bags of dog food were all the owner wanted.

He told the hunter that Webster wasn't much of a hunting dog; he was too small and couldn't keep up with the other dogs. The hunter already knew that, so he thanked the owner and told Webster to hop in his truck.

Webster was so excited!

Webster loved his new home. The hunter fed him twice a day and he even had his very own food bowl. He didn't have to worry about fighting the other dogs to get a scrap of food anymore.

At night, Webster snuggled into his very own bed. He had gone from the **pen to the penthouse!**

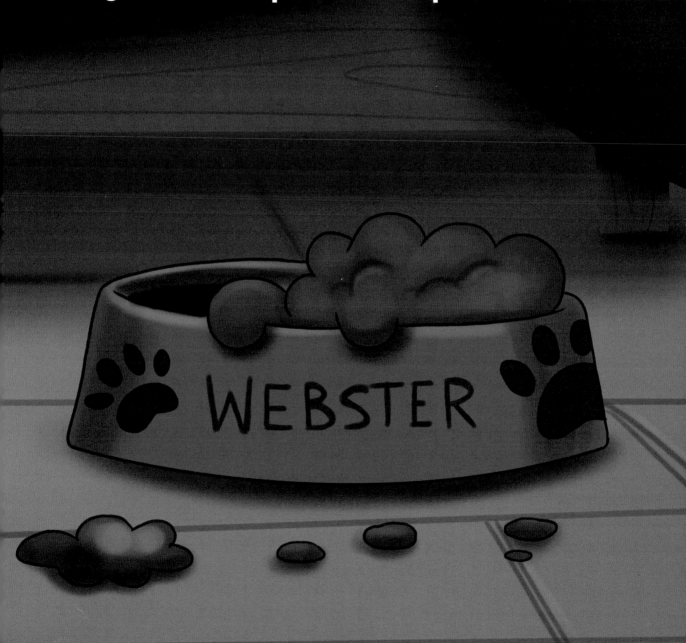

Webster's favorite part of his new family was his new brother and sister. And they were so delighted with him, they took him everywhere.

Before long, Webster's family noticed that everyone wanted to be around him— children, adults, and even other dogs.

That's when they realized they had to share Webster's special brand of joy with those who needed it most. Webster was going to be a therapy dog!

After training and certification, Webster donned his training dog vest and was off to local nursing homes, rehab centers, and hospitals with his family. He was a natural.

Sometimes Webster wore doggy costumes and performed for the crowds, getting lots of laughs and applause. Webster's weekly visits were the brightest and best parts of the day for a lot of folks, including Webster!

One of Webster's favorite spots to visit with his family was the local children's hospital. It was there where he let the children run their hands through his fur or scratch his belly. When he saw how happy the kids were when they petted him, Webster knew he had a special job and he was happy to do it.

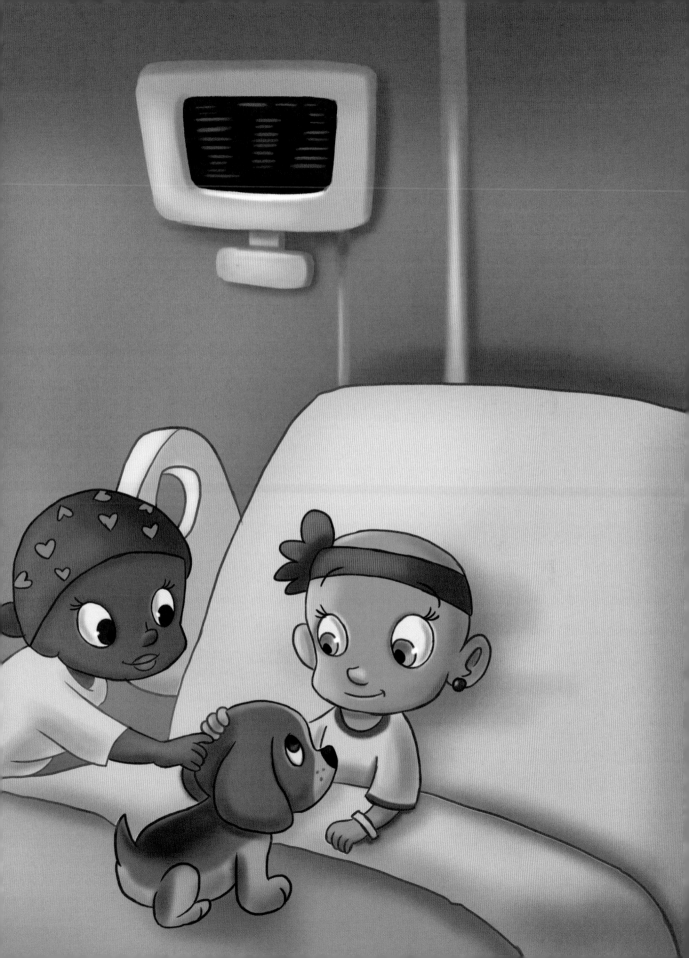

Webster's family loved it too. Everywhere they took him, they told the story of how Webster had gone from a sad hunting dog who was lost in the woods to a happy therapy dog who had found his family.

Everyone who heard his story was inspired and full of hope. Webster taught them to never give up on their dreams.

Every night when Webster
went to sleep in his new home,
he smiled. He knew he was
the best hunter in the world
because he had caught the
best family!

About the Author

Frank's energy and enthusiasm for life are contagious, so it's no wonder dog breeds such as beagles and Labradors are a perfect fit for him. He is an avid hunter, tennis player, and fan of all things James Madison University. Frank is also active in his community, and enjoys exploring new ventures from owning racehorses to oyster farming.

Frank lives in Richmond, Virginia, with his wife, Caren, and their two dogs, Deacon, a rescued beagle, and River, a black Labrador retriever. This is his first children's book.